THEY'RE FAMOUSE . . .
THEY'RE FABUMOUSE . . .
AND THE[...]
TO SAVE [...]
THEY'RE THE

HEROMICE

AND THESE ARE THEIR
ADVENTURES!

D0769829

Geronimo Stilton

HEROMICE

INSECT INVASION

Scholastic Inc.

If you purchased this book without a cover, you should be aware that this book is stolen property. It was reported as "unsold and destroyed" to the publisher, and neither the author nor the publisher has received any payment for this "stripped book."

Copyright © 2015 by Edizioni Piemme S.p.A., Palazzo Mondadori, Via Mondadori 1, 20090 Segrate, Italy. International Rights © Atlantyca S.p.A. English translation © 2017 by Atlantyca S.p.A.

The publisher does not have any control over and does not assume any responsibility for author or third-party websites or their content.

GERONIMO STILTON names, characters, and related indicia are copyright, trademark, and exclusive license of Atlantyca S.p.A. All rights reserved. The moral right of the author has been asserted. Based on an original idea by Elisabetta Dami. www.geronimostilton.com

Published by Scholastic Inc., *Publishers since 1920*, 557 Broadway, New York, NY 10012. SCHOLASTIC and associated logos are trademarks and/or registered trademarks of Scholastic Inc.

Stilton is the name of a famous English cheese. It is a registered trademark of the Stilton Cheese Makers' Association. For more information, go to www.stiltoncheese.com.

No part of this publication may be reproduced, stored in a retrieval system, or transmitted in any form or by any means, electronic, mechanical, photocopying, recording, or otherwise without written permission of the copyright holder. For information regarding permission, please contact: Atlantyca S.p.A., Via Leopardi 8, 20123 Milan, Italy; e-mail foreignrights@atlantyca.it, www.atlantyca.com.

This book is a work of fiction. Names, characters, places, and incidents are either the product of the author's imagination or are used fictitiously, and any resemblance to actual persons, living or dead, business establishments, events, or locales is entirely coincidental.

ISBN 978-1-338-11661-8

Text by Geronimo Stilton
Original title *S.O.S. superinsetti all'assalto*
Original design of the Heromice world by Giuseppe Facciotto and Flavio Ferron
Cover by Giuseppe Facciotto (design) and Daniele Verzini (color)
Illustrations by Luca Usai (pencils), Valeria Cairoli (inks), and Serena Gianoli and Daniele Verzini (color)
Graphics by Francesca Sirianni and Chiara Cebraro

Special thanks to Shannon Penney
Translated by Andrea Schaffer
Interior design by Kevin Callahan/BNGO Books

10 9 8 7 6 5 4 3 2   17 18 19 20 21

Printed in the U.S.A.   40

First printing 2017

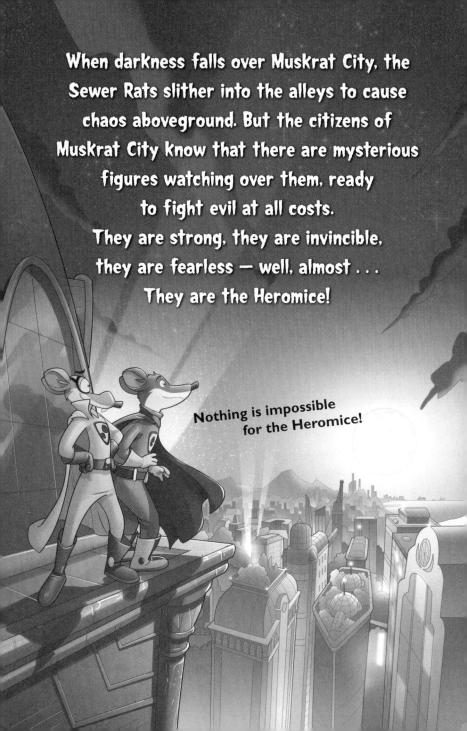

When darkness falls over Muskrat City, the Sewer Rats slither into the alleys to cause chaos aboveground. But the citizens of Muskrat City know that there are mysterious figures watching over them, ready to fight evil at all costs.
They are strong, they are invincible, they are fearless — well, almost . . .
They are the Heromice!

Nothing is impossible for the Heromice!

MEET THE HEROMICE!

GERONIMO SUPERSTILTON

The strongest hero in Muskrat City . . . but he still must learn how to control his powers!

SWIFTPAWS

Geronimo Superstilton's partner in crimefighting; he can transform his supersuit into anything.

LADY WONDERWHISKERS

A mysterious mouse with special powers; she always seems to be in the right place at the right time.

TESS TECHNOPAWS

A cook and scientist who assists the Heromice with every mission.

ELECTRON AND PROTON

Supersmart mouselets who help the Heromice; they create and operate sophisticated technological gadgets.

TONY SLUDGE

The undisputed leader of the Sewer Rats; known for being tough and mean.

TERESA SLUDGE

SLICKFUR

Tony's wife; makes the important decisions for their family.

Sludge's right-hand mouse; the true (and only) brains behind the Sewer Rats.

ELENA SLUDGE

ONE, TWO, AND THREE

Tony and Teresa's teenage daughter; has a real weakness for rat metal music.

Bodyguards who act as Sludge's henchmice; they are big, buff, and brainless.

THE BIG GAME!

One beautiful **spring** day, I scurried home after work, my whiskers trembling with excitement. The **RODENT SPORTS NETWORK** was showing my favorite soccer team's big game!

I wouldn't miss seeing the Parmesan City Pawbreakers in action for all the cheese in New Mouse City. I couldn't wait to see how many **goals** their captain, Gary Goalmouse, would score. He was one of the most fabumouse players in the whole world!

Oops, sorry—I haven't introduced myself! My name is Stilton, *Geronimo Stilton*, and I'm the editor of *The Rodent's Gazette*, the most famous **newspaper** on Mouse Island.

As I was saying, I **hurried** to my mouse hole, filled an enormouse bowl with Parmesan popcorn, turned on the **TEAKETTLE**, and sat down in front of the TV.

I had just settled into my favorite chair, with a blanket on my lap and the remote control in my paw, when . . .

Riiiing! Riiiing!

Cheese and crackers, the telephone rang just as the BiG Game was about to start. Squeak!

I stood up to answer it, but I tripped on the rug and — **BAM!**

Oof!

I landed snoutdown in my popcorn. Holey cheese, what a mess!

"Geronimo? Are you there?" I heard the voice of my friend Hercule Poirat coming from the phone.

I scrambled to grab the receiver. "Yes, but—"

"**Super Swiss slices**, we need you in Muskrat City right away! There's a super-emergency!"

I didn't like the sound of that! "**SUPER-EMERGENCY?**"

"The city is in danger!" Hercule squeaked. "They need the Heromice!"

"I've told you a thousand times—*I'm not cut out to be a Heromouse!*" I muttered. "But I guess I don't have a choice. When a friend calls, I have to respond."

Hercule cheered. "I knew I could count on you! See you soon, partner!"

Then he hung up.

Cheese niblets! **W** **H** **Y** does this sort of thing always happen to me?

The game was about to begin, but Hercule—otherwise known by his Heromouse name, Swiftpaws—was waiting for me in Muʃkrat City. I couldn't leave him hanging! Moldy mozzarella, sometimes it was hard to be such an upstanding mouse.

So I **reluctantly** turned off the TV, took out my Superpen, and pressed the tiny hidden button on the clip. A bright green **superlaser** appeared, instantly transforming me into **SUPERSTILTON**!

Sigh . . .

With no time to lose, I leaped out the window at supersonic speed.

Squeak! Flying always frightened me out of my fur!

I looked for something to cling to, but the only thing in my paws was the wool BLANKet that had been covering my lap. Rats! What good would that do me?

As if that wasn't bad enough, the sky was full of dark clouds!

I found myself inside a cloud as **black** as the belly of a cat. Lightning singed my whiskers and toasted my tail.

"HELLLLLLLLLPPPPPPP!" I cried. But there was no one to save me. After all, I was the Heromouse!

INSIDE THE MYSTERIOUS TUNNEL

As I struggled in the superstorm, my cape—and the blanket—got soaked with RAIN. Soon they were as heavy as giant wheels of aged cheddar! They weighed me down, down, down. I plummeted toward the roofs of Muskrat City!

Oh no! I was gone, done for, a dead mouse!

"I don't want to splat on the ground like a Heromouse meatball!" I cried.

When I was just a few tails from the ground, I heard someone holler:

"Supersuit: Super-Trampoline Mode!"

I opened my eyes and looked down. **Swiftpaws** was there, and he had transformed himself into a fantastic, elastic trampoline!

At the *very last second*, I bounced on the trampoline with a powerful

Great Gouda, what a super-relief!

As I **BOUNCED** back up into the sky, I yelled, "Th-thanks, Swiftpaws! You're a true friend!"

But a few seconds later, I was falling again!

"NOOOOOOO!"

I cried, looking down. Below me was a big hole . . .

. . . and I landed right in it!

"Help!"

I began to roll down, down, down toward the center of the earth. It seemed like the hole would never end!

Was it a mouse hole?

A MINE SHAFT?

A SUBTERRANEAN TUNNEL?

It was impossible to say—I couldn't see a thing down there, not even my own snout!

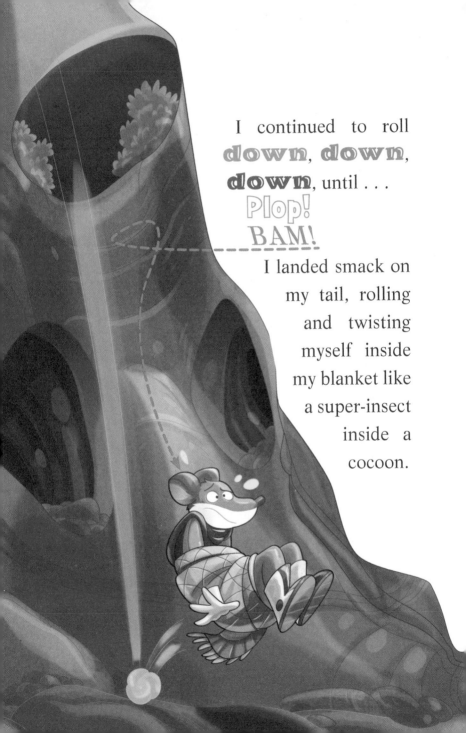

I continued to roll **down**, **down**, **down**, until . . .

Plop!
BAM!

I landed smack on my tail, rolling and twisting myself inside my blanket like a super-insect inside a cocoon.

Owwwwwww! What superpain!
A second later, a DAZZLING light hit me
square in the snout. What on Earth
could it be?

"**Super Swiss slices**,
Superstilton! Welcome!"
said Swiftpaws, ZEROING
in on me with his
headlamp. "What are
you doing inside that
blanket? You're

Welcome,
partner!

Squeak!
Turn off that light!

not planning to take a nap, *are you*?"

I tried to cover my eyes with the blanket.

"Uh . . . I . . . wait a second!" I squeaked. "Where are we?"

"In a tunnel created by gnawing super-insects that have invaded the city," Swiftpaws responded promptly.

"Gnawing s-s-s-super-insects?!" I didn't want to believe my ears!

"I told you there was a super-emergency!" Swiftpaws said. "These things came out of nowhere and started chewing on everything: pavement, benches, houses, even lampposts."

I gulped. "B-but what can we do about it?"

"We can stop them!" Swiftpaws replied. "It'll be easy-cheesy for us Heromice. After all, they're just giant insects!"

Before Swiftpaws could say anything else,

a **BUZZING NOISE** drowned out his voice. A moment later, a swarm of insects appeared in the air—and they were headed right toward us!

A HEROIC ESCAPE!

I was shaking in my fur—those were the loudest insects I'd ever heard! They also had **SUPER-POINTY** legs and **super-spiky** pincers . . . gasp! And *supersharp* teeth . . . argh!

Swiftpaws leaped into action, yelling, *"Supersuit: Flypaper Mode!"*

The insects swooped down close to us, but they were instantly **TRAPPED** in Swiftpaws's cape, which had transformed

into **sticky** yellow flypaper!

"Um, Swiftpaws, are you SURE this is a good idea?" I squeaked.

His only response was, "Ow! Ouch! Eeek! Ooo! Superstilton, *hellllllppppp*!"

Now that he had trapped them, Swiftpaws couldn't get those ANNOYING insects off of him! They were stuck to his supersuit, and they were BiTiNG him all over! Mighty mozzarella, what was I supposed to do?

"For all the cheddar in Muskrat City!" I cried. "Hold on, Swiftpaws! I'm coming!"

Before I knew what was happening, my cheesy powers activated. A shower of

cheddar cheese chunks poured down!

BOING! BOING! BOING! BOING!

The *sudden cheesestorm* surprised the gnawing insects, and they flew away. Holey cheese, what a close call!

"Thanks, partner," Swiftpaws said. He looked at his munched-up cape and sighed. "Cosmic cheddar, what a disaster!"

But that was the least of our problems, because — bzzzzzzzzzz! — the insects were coming back to attack again!

Swiftpaws squeaked:

"Supersuit: Super-Pinwheel Mode!"

I held up my paws. "No, no, no! You know I'm afraid of heights! I'm just a regular rodent. I'm not cut out to be a Heromouse!"

"Be strong, Superstilton!" Swiftpaws

cried. "We have to get back to **Heromice Headquarters**!"

Next thing I knew, we were flying through the air. *SQUEEEEEEEAK!*

Be strong, Superstilton!

Aaaaaaaahhhh!

WHO'S SCARED OF CRICKETS?

When we landed safely at Heromice Headquarters, Tess Technopaws welcomed us with a huge tray of delicious cheesy **treats**. As *QUICK* as a cat, Swiftpaws gobbled:

4 mozzarella muffins with fondue icing,

3 chocolate cheesecakes with sprinkles, and

1 whole teapot of hot cheddar tea.

I had to be happy with what

was left on the **TRAY**—a muffin and a cheesecake. Oh, well. They were still **whisker-licking** good!

Besides, there was no time to lose. Our fabumouse team was waiting for us!

As soon as we entered the **control room**, Electron greeted us with a grin. "Welcome, Heromice!"

Proton waved and got right down to business. "We've been trying to find out more about the giant insects that have invaded the city."

"And what have you learned about those destructive cheesebrains?" Swiftpaws asked with a scowl. "They totally shredded my supersuit!"

"We know that they're **crickets**, and they love to devour things," Electron explained. "But we haven't discovered much else yet, since they're pretty rare in Muskrat City."

Suddenly, Tess entered the Control Room with a sewing basket in one paw. "Don't worry, Swiftpaws. Just a few stitches and your cape will be as good as new!"

Swiftpaws's eyes widened. "Super Swiss slices! Isn't there a **FASTER** way?"

Tess smiled **mysteriously**. "I'm working on one . . . but for now, you'll have to make do with a needle and thread!"

Swiftpaws sighed and went to work. Meanwhile, Electron pressed a button and a map of Muskrat City appeared on the control room's main screen. **Red lights** glowed all over the map.

Electron said, "This locator is a digital device that can recognize the **frequencies** emitted by the insects."

"LOCATOR? DIGITAL DEVICE? FREQUENCIES?"
I repeated. Great Gouda globs, my head was spinning!

I didn't understand A SINGLE THING Electron was squeaking about, so I asked, "But what are those little *lights*?"

"The crickets!" Electron responded.

Everyone stared at the screen. Our jaws hung open like stretchy string cheese left out in the sun. **Cosmic cheddar chunks!** There were so many of them!

Suddenly, the lights began to move toward the center of the city, creating one big flashing red spot on the screen.

Proton and Electron both squeaked, "They're headed for Swiss Square!"

"Holey cheese!" I cried. "They're going to attack the center of the city!"

Swiftpaws leaped to his paws. "There's no time to lose! We must stop them and save Muskrat City!"

I hated to admit it, but the idea of getting my fur too close to those CRICKETS and their sharp fangs made my whiskers wobble!

I stuttered, "W-well, I think th-that f-first

we need to r-rest a little bit . . . and f-f-finish patching Swiftpaws's cape . . ."

Swiftpaws shook his snout. "This cape won't stop me, **PaRtneR**!" He bolted for the door.

Mighty mozzarella—I had no choice but to **follow** him!

Supersonic Accelerators!

We headed out as fast as our paws would take us, but a voice stopped us in our tracks. "Hey, Heromice—hold up!"

It was **Tess**. She had the sewing basket over one arm.

"We're in a hurry, Tess!" Swiftpaws replied impatiently. "Patching my cape can wait."

But Tess started rummaging through scissors, balls of yarn, and colorful spools of thread. **"Cosmic cheesy chews**, I was sure they were in here," she muttered.

She set the basket down on a table, adjusted her glasses, and began to

pull out a series of objects:
- a **ball** of wool
- a pair of *pliers*
- a kitchen apron
- a portable microscope
- three spoons
- and a magnifying **lens**.

Ummm...

Where are they?

Huh?!

"Aha!" she cried triumphantly. "Here they are! They were buried at the bottom of the basket."

She held up two shiny fabric bands that were studded with rhinestones.

"Belts?" asked Swiftpaws, scratching his snout in confusion. "But what are they for?"

Tess smiled. "These aren't belts, dear. These are SUPERSONIC ACCELERATORS, and they're one of my latest inventions." Before I could twitch a whisker, she had fastened one of the strange **bands** around my waist.

"Are you ready, Superstilton?"

"Um, that depends . . ." I said cautiously.

"Hold on to your tail!" was Tess's reply.

"Wait a second!" I squeaked. "WHat's GoinG to HaPPen?"

She responded with a wink.

Now my whiskers were trembling with fear. "For the love of cheese, could someone please tell me what's going on?"

"Don't worry," TESS whispered sweetly. "It's going to be okay, dear. I programmed the Supersonic Accelerator myself. It will bring you to your destination safe and sound!"

She pressed a RED button, then a YELLOW one, then a GREEN one, and—

SWOOOSHHH!

Two rockets ignited on the sides of the belt! By the power of Parmesan—I suddenly

Squeeeeaak!

blasted off at full speed.

"HEEELLLP!"

I squeaked as I flew into the air.

When I finally worked up the courage to open my eyes, I saw Swiftpaws flying next to me, wearing the other belt. "Super Swiss slices!" he cried. "This belt isn't half bad!"

But I could only think of one thing: "How do we get **dooooown**?"

While we hurtled at supersonic speed over Muskrat City, I began to randomly press the buttons on my Supersonic Accelerator.

Aaaaaahhh!

The **first** button made me do a somersault. The **SECOND** turned off the accelerator completely. I found myself free-falling over the roofs of the city!

Luckily, the *third* button relit the rockets at maximum power. **Whew!** I'm too fond of my fur!

But now I had a new problem. "I don't know how to stop!"

"What do you mean, cheesebrain?" Swiftpaws said. "Just pull on the brake."

"**BRAKE?**" I squeaked. "This thing has a brake?"

Hellllllppppp!

Just then, I noticed a hidden lever on one **edge** of the belt. *Why hadn't anyone told me sooner?*

Wait for me!
Here I come!

I **pulled** hard on the lever, and—

Screeeeech!

I landed on the ground with a thud. My boots skidded along the whole length of the square as I tried to stop!

Luckily, no one was paying attention to me—they were all too busy looking at something else.

Gulp!

It works — phew!

Before me was a swarm of crickets, **hopping** and smacking their jaws. But this time, the insects were not alone. They carried a stretcher with a kind of throne on top. A **masked** creature sat there. He looked so mean, my fur stood on end!

THE MASKED RODENT

"Super Swiss slices!" Swiftpaws yelled. "Do you **SEE** that, Superstilton?"

The creature on the throne wore a dark mask with two speakers where his ears should have been. Cheese and crackers, how strange! Despite the bizarre look, there was something **familiar** about him.

Suddenly . . .

"BWAHAHAHAHA!"

The masked rodent's laughter echoed around the plaza, making my whiskers WOBBLE with fear!

While my knees shook like **cottage cheese**, Swiftpaws hollered, "**Who** are you and **W H A T** do you want?"

The scary masked creature repeated, "Bwahahaha! Who I am isn't important, but what I can do is! At my signal, the **crickets** will begin to devour Muskrat City. Soon, it will just be a pile of **dust**!"

"Ugh, these insects have got to go!" Swiftpaws **groaned**, turning to me. "Am I right, partner? Hey, Superstilton?"

I knew I should have said something, but I was as **petrified** as a chunk of super-stale cheddar. I couldn't even squeak!

How many times do I have to say it? I'm not cut out to be a Heromouse!

The masked rodent glared at us. "Here's what you must do, superfools! Paw over the keys to the city—and a lifetime supply of

gooey GOUDA! If you don't, Muskrat City will be chewed, **CRUSHED**, and reduced to **rubble**!"

"I've had enough of this!" Swiftpaws replied. "We won't stand for your threats.

HeRomice in action!"

UNMASKED!

Swiftpaws raised one paw in the air.

"Supersuit: Super-Perfume Mode!" he squeaked

He suddenly transformed into an enormouse bottle shaped like a beautiful FLOWER. An instant later, he began to spray an irresistible perfume from the center of the flower to attract the crickets.

All of the insects TURNED toward Swiftpaws, cocking their antennae.

Come here, icky insects!

"*Hee, hee, hee!* It's the perfect plan!" he exclaimed. "Hey, Superstilton, am I or am I not a SUPERGENIUS?"

The insects that supported the stretcher moved toward the perfume, and the masked rodent swung dangerously on his perch. "Hey!" he cried. "Stay put, crickets!"

"Come, insects! Come on, come on, come on—follow me!" Swiftpaws called.

TRIK! TRIK!! TRIK!!!

The crickets began to sharpen their PINCERS. Mighty mozzarella, it was really loud!

"Uh, Swiftpaws?" I said. I suddenly had a bad feeling about this. "I think they want to—um, it seems like they're about to—"

But I was too late. The super-insects were already LAUNCHING themselves at my partner! Soon, he was covered with bites.

Blistering blue cheese, I had to do something!

Swiftpaws **bolted away**, trying to escape the swarm of crickets.
"HEEEEELP!"

Some of the crickets had started to munch on my cape, too! **By the power of Parmesan**, what could I do?!

I knew one thing for sure — I couldn't leave Swiftpaws alone. So I took a step forward and tried to **SWAT** the insects with my paws. But there were too many!

I could hear the masked creature laughing. **"Bwahahahahaha!"**

"I don't know what to do, Swiftpaws!" I yelled in frustration. "**FOr a thOuSaND CHuNKS OF CHeDDar**, there are so many of them!"

With those words, my cheesy superpowers accidentally activated again, and a shower of delicious cheddar chunks **poured** down on Swiftpaws and the crickets. SHOCKED, the insects leaped away in a flash!

BonK!

Chunks of cheese also hit the strange creature on the head. His mask bounced off and slipped to the ground.

SUPERPOWER: SHOWER OF CHEDDAR CHUNKS ACTIVATED WITH THE CRY: "FOR A THOUSAND CHUNKS OF CHEDDAR!"

"It's Slickfur!" exclaimed Swiftpaws. "He was the rat hidden behind the MASK!"

It really was Slickfur! He was the slimy henchmouse to **Tony Sludge**, leader of the Sewer Rats.

Suddenly, the crickets

Ack!

stopped attacking us. Some snored *tranquilly*, while others hopped here and there, and others dug holes in the ground.

Wait one whisker-loving minute!

Slickfur? The crickets? The strange mask with the speakers?

Of course!

Slickfur's mask must have been a type of mega–remote control. He had been using it to control the crickets!

It made perfect sense!

As soon as the mask fell to the ground, the crickets went back to being regular old jumping insects.

I knew what I had to do. Quiet as a mouse, I tried to grab the mask—but I was **too late**!

Slickfur snagged the mask in his paw before I could reach it! Then he turned

We'll be back!

a knob, and the crickets gathered quickly around him. As they all flew up into the 𝕊𝕜𝕪, Slickfur called

"This isn't the end, superfools!"

He's escaping!

Oh no!

THE MOUSETASTIC
RADIO MASK

There was nothing to do but return to Heromice Headquarters. We needed advice from our friends!

Swiftpaws and I walked into headquarters with our capes trailing behind us. They'd been completely munched up by super-crickets, and now they had more holes than two slices of Swiss!

"We'll worry about the your capes later, Heromice!" Electron said. "We've confirmed that the Sewer Rats developed a mousetastic radio mask that they can use to command the insects."

Proton added, "We're connected to the security cameras in the different stores around Swiss Square, so we got a photo of Slickfur's mask."

A model of the mask appeared on the screen on the wall.

"You see those two SPEAKERS in place of ears?" Electron asked.

I squinted at the model carefully.

"The speakers play certain frequencies

Do you see those?

Oooh . . .

that Slickfur uses to communicate with the crickets," Electron continued.

"Supersonic Swiss!" Swiftpaws squeaked. "So all we have to do is get rid of the mask!"

"Exactly!" Electron said. "But first, we need to do something about your ruined capes, right?"

Swiftpaws and I nodded. Our supersuits looked worse than moldy cheese chunks!

"I know how to make them as good as new," Tess said with a wink. She opened a nearby cabinet and pulled out something that looked like a hand-crank pasta maker. Holey cheese, what was it?

"Here's the Electromagnetic Cut-and-Sew machine I invented for just this sort of thing!" Tess announced.

She stuck my cape into the machine and

began to **TURN** the crank.

The cape passed through the roller and came out looking like new. By the power of Parmesan, it was amazing!

"You're FABUMOUSE, Tess!" I cried. "Thank you!"

But as Tess put Swiftpaws's **CAPE** into the machine, an alarm sounded in the control room.

"Hurry, Heromice!" Electron exclaimed. "We're getting an emergency call from **Commissioner Ratford**!"

Swiftpaws and I raced over to the supercomputer, and the police chief of Muskrat City appeared on the screen. Cheese niblets, he really seemed to have his tail in a twist!

"Heromice, we have a problem!" the commissioner said. "The crickets have just attacked the big dam on the Muskrat City River!"

"How?" Swiftpaws asked, tugging on his whiskers.

"They're eating the dam!" the commissioner squeaked. "We have to hurry—I don't know how long it will hold. If we don't stop those insects in time, the whole city will be **flooded**!"

Swiftpaws grabbed his cape from the Electromagnetic Cut-and-Sew machine and ran out the door.

"Heromice in action!"

he cried.

I followed right on his tail.

Just outside headquarters, Swiftpaws cried, "Supersuit: Instant Ejection Seat Mode!"

Before I could shake my snout, I found myself sitting in a yellow airplane seat, ready for takeoff!

"S-STOP, SWIFTPAWS! YOU DON'T REALLY—"

But all I heard was a **BOING** and a **SWOOSH** as we flew at supersonic speed toward the *dam*.

Aaaaargh!

MORE HOLES THAN A SLICE OF SWISS!

Luckily, the dam wasn't far, and we got there in a flash! Swiftpaws landed on the ground with an *agile* and **ATHLETIC** leap, just like a real Heromouse. I, on the other paw, landed with my snout in a *puddle*!

The crickets were chomping away at the wall of the dam. They seemed to have an **endless** appetite! (Just like me when there's cheesecake on the table . . .)

Their pincers, fangs, and claws had already made an enormouse **hole** in the dam — and a cascade of **water** was pouring through!

We had to do something **quickly**!

Swiftpaws leaped into action.

"Supersuit: Cork Mode!"

Let's go!

Before I could blink, he transformed into a large **YELLOW** cork, ready to plug the hole in the dam. I stood, frozen in my fur, until Swiftpaws hollered, "Be brave, SUPERSTILTON! Come give me a paw!"

"I'm coming!" I said meekly, my tail trembling with fear.

I did my best to plug a few of the smaller holes in the dam, blocking them with my paws. How mousetastically **EXHAUSTING**!

As I scrambled around the dam, some

crickets started to get dangerously CLOSE to me. No! I'm too fond of my fur!

"HELLLLPPPP!"

I closed my eyes, preparing for the **worst**, when . . .

SWOOOOSHHH!

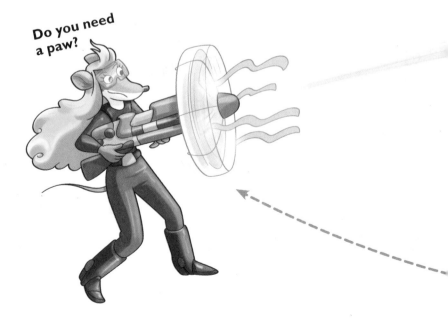

Do you need a paw?

A gust of **wind** overpowered the super-insects. Then the unmistakable scent of **Gruyere No. 5** perfume spread through

Bzzzz . . .

Bzzzzzzz!

the air. A second later, I saw her — the fabumouse, incredible, truly super **Lady Wonderwhiskers**.

"Do you need a paw, Heromice?" she asked us. She was holding a SUPER-FAN in one paw.

59

It's Raining Mozzarella!

Lady Wonderwhiskers, the Heromouse of my **heart**, was graceful and elegant. Me, on the other paw? My fur was **matted**, my tail was twisted, and my whiskers were trembling. All I could squeak was, "I'm losing my balaaaaance!"

"Hold on, Superstilton!" Lady Wonderwhiskers said.

"*FOR A THOUSAND BALLS OF MOZZARELLA!*" I cried, frightened out of my fur.

PLOP PLOP PLOP PLOP PLOP PLOP PLOP PLOP PLOP PLOP PLOP PLOP PLOP PLOP PLOP PLOP PLOP

With those words, my amazing cheesy superpowers activated, and a thousand balls of soft mozzarella showered down on the DAM!

Lady Wonderwhiskers squeaked, "I have an idea—let's use the mozzarella balls to plug the **HOLES** in the dam!"

Great cheese chunks, **what a smarty-mouse**!

We quickly gathered the balls of

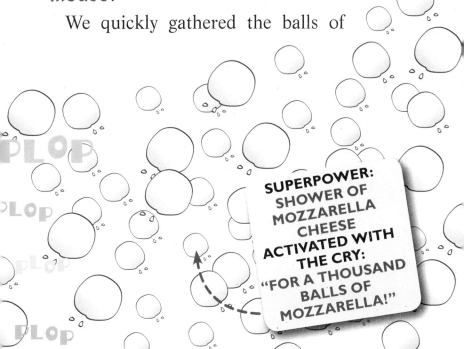

PLOP

PLOP

PLOP

PLOP

SUPERPOWER: SHOWER OF MOZZARELLA CHEESE ACTIVATED WITH THE CRY: "FOR A THOUSAND BALLS OF MOZZARELLA!"

mozzarella and began to use them as delicious, delicious plugs. I had to use all my superstrength not to gobble them up!

BZ

BZZZ!

BZZZ

BZ

BZZZZZZZZZ!

BZZZz!

BZZZZZZZz!

BZZZZZZ

Here we go . . .

BZZZZZZZZZ

BZZ

Fixed!

BZ

BZZZZZZZZZz!

BZZZZ!

Perfect!

BZZZZZZZ!

BZZZZ!

Swiftpaws
said **cheerfully**,
"Good work,
Superstilton! Your
mozzarella balls arrived just in time!"

My **superpartner** tossed a ball of
mozzarella in the air and caught it in his
mouth. "**Yum!** Tasty."

But a second later . . .

The **crickets** were
back and **BUZZING**!

Slickfur was urging

them along from behind his mask.

"We have to get that mask away from him!" Swiftpaws exclaimed.

"Supersuit: Super-Magnet Mode!"

Come to me, mask!

Swiftpaws transformed into an enormouse yellow-and-red **magnet**! He approached Slickfur, but at the last minute, a swarm of crickets made him stumble. Great Gouda globs, he'd been so close to snagging the mask!

"Bwahahahahaha!" Tony Sludge's **malicious** henchmouse sneered. "Surrender now, superfools!"

But Lady Wonderwhiskers and Swiftpaws stood side by side, looking SUPER-TOUGH!

64

I joined them.

"Heromice to the rescue!"

we all squeaked together.

Slickfur didn't waste a moment! He used the mask to let out a *loud* call: three short buzzes and a very long whistle.

Bzzz! Bzzz! Bzzz!

Before I could twitch a whisker, the crickets all left the dam and flew over to Slickfur. Then, a **chasm** opened up beneath them! The super-insects and Slickfur disappeared, leaving behind only a cloud of dust.

As soon as the cloud CLEARED, I realized that Lady Wonderwhiskers had also disappeared. Super Swiss slices, had they taken her prisoner?

"We have to follow them!" Swiftpaws said.

My partner ran for the gigantic open

chasm in the **EARTH**, waving a paw for me to follow.

I shook my snout. "I'm not going down there!"

"Superstilton, don't be a 'FRAIDY MOUSE!" he cried. "We have to do it!"

Riiing! Riiing! Riiing!

It was my **HEROMOUSE** watch! When I answered, I could see Proton and **ELECTRON** on the screen, calling me from Heromice Headquarters.

"Superstilton! Swiftpaws!" Electron squeaked. "You Can't let them get away!"

"**N-N-NO**, I'm not going down there!" I stuttered. "It could be dangerous! It could be a trap! We could hurt ourselves!"

"Calm down," Proton said. "Tess has already thought of this."

Hmmm . . . what in the name of all things cheesy could that mean?

TESS'S SLICK FIX

I never knew what kind of fabumouse new invention to expect from Tess, and this time she had really taken the cheese. **ELECTRON** appeared on my Heromouse watch screen. "Touch your capes, Heromice!"

I pressed my cape and—*how strange*!

I can see myself!

Wow!

It seemed different than usual, as if it had been made from something smooth and GUMMY.

"When Tess put your capes through the Electromagnetic Cut-and-Sew machine, she also applied

68

a special layer of *Slick Fix*," Electron squeaked. "With this mousetastic, supersmooth coating, you'll be able to slip through the tunnel like it's a soapy floor!"

"**MOUSERIFIC!**" Swiftpaws cheered.

But I wasn't so sure. I peeked into the tunnel again. It was so big and dark — anything could be lurking down there! I don't like being in mysterious places where you can't see the ends of your own whiskers . . .

Proton squeaked, "Hurry, Heromice! We're counting on you!"

SWIFTPAWS was ready to leap into the bottomless tunnel.

"Have courage, Superstilton!" he said, squeezing my PAW. "On three, let's close our eyes and jump together!"

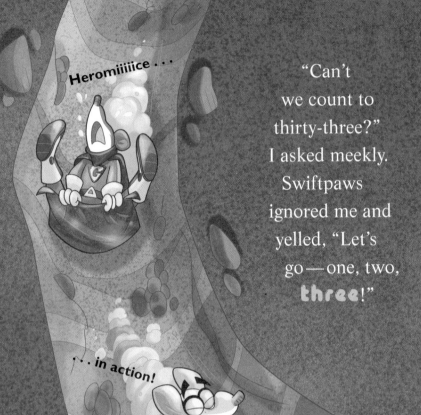

"Can't we count to thirty-three?" I asked meekly. Swiftpaws ignored me and yelled, "Let's go—one, two, **three**!"

Rat-munching rattlesnakes, I wasn't ready! But we leaped into the dark tunnel anyway, yelling,

"HEROMICE IN ACTION!"

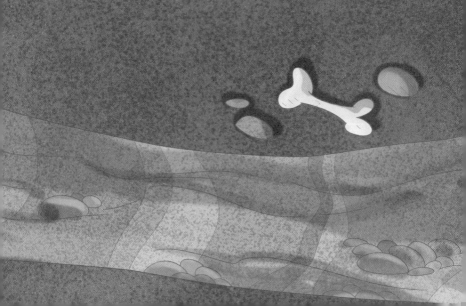

THE SECRET PASSAGE

Thanks to Tess's **Slick Fix**, we slid through the deep tunnel at supersonic speed.

HOLEY CHEESE!

"You can't see your own snout in here!" I yelped. "**Why** does this sort of thing always happen to meeeeeeee?"

After what seemed like forever — **KERPLUNK!** We finally landed . . . in a stinky puddle.

"Welcome to the **sewer**, partner!" Swiftpaws said cheerfully, wringing the muddy water out of his **cape**.

Rats! My superboots were full of water that smelled worse than rancid cottage cheese. I emptied them with one paw, plugging my snout with the other.

Yuck!

"Now what do we do?" I asked. "It's so **DARK** in here, we couldn't tell a cat from a rat!"

"You said it!" Swiftpaws laughed. "So let's turn on the lights. What do you say, Superstilton?"

Swiftpaws's supersuit activated and **illuminated** the tunnel ahead of us. Cosmic cheddar chunks! Now we could see an underground plaza full of *rusty* and **dripping** pipes.

My whiskers trembled. "But this is a

LABYRINTH! We'll never find Slickfur or the crickets in this maze!"

Swiftpaws shrugged. "We have to start somewhere, right? Let's go that way." He pointed down a tunnel to the left. It was full of stinky slime. Yuck!

But . . .

Let's go, partner!

After just a few steps . . . **Look!**

"And here we are!" Swiftpaws cried. "Well what did I tell you, Superstilton?"

"**HUH?**" I asked. What in the world was he squeaking about?

Swiftpaws pointed at a small stone. "Doesn't it seem strange that this pebble is coming out of the wall? It must be connected to a **secret passage!**"

Swiftpaws pushed the stone with all his might and the wall began to move! Mighty mozzarella, I couldn't believe it!

I stepped forward to take a better look. Squeak! It really was a **secret passage!**

Maybe it would lead us to the fortress of Rottington, the hideout of the *Sewer Rats*!

"Nice work, Swiftp—"

But I didn't finish my sentence in time.

KLACK!

The wall spun around.

Then . . . **SCREECH!**

A large net released from the ceiling.

And . . . **ziP!**

Holey cheese—the net tightened around our paws! My **partner** and I found ourselves hanging snouts-down, like melting Muenster ice cream!

"Super Swiss!" Swiftpaws whispered. "Maybe I was wrong about that."

I tore at my whiskers. "Maybe? **MAYBE?**"

Swiftpaws shrugged. "Can you move over? You're squishing me."

"**YOU** move over!" I squeaked, twisting my tail. "Your supersuit smells like a super-stinky triple-slime smoothie!"

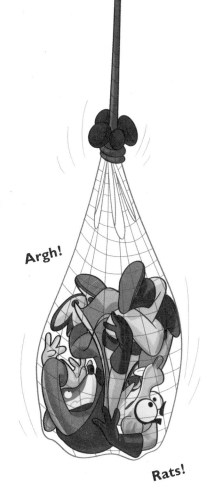

Argh!

Rats!

"Shhhhh!" Swiftpaws held a paw to his lips. "Remember that we're on a secret mission, Superstilton."

I sighed. For the love of cheese, there was no reasoning with my partner!

"What secret mission?" I asked. "This net is a *trap*!"

We had been total superfools. The Sewer Rats had known that we would be coming, and they had welcomed us with open paws . . . right into their *trap*! How do I always get myself into these messes?

Inside the
Broom Closet

Swiftpaws and I tried EVERYTHING we could think of to get out of the net.

"Let's try to swing it back and forth," my partner said, rocking the net.

"Stop, Swiftpaws!" I groaned. "You're making me motion sick!"

"Okay, I'll just try one quick swing," he responded. "Hold on!"

The net swung so hard that we did a double-somersault! Squeak!

I felt more mixed-up than a mozzarella milkshake!

Before my head even stopped spinning, a noise rang out in the tunnel. It sounded like pawsteps!

"Who goes there?" asked Swiftpaws.

There was no answer.

The steps came **closer** and **closer** until **ONE** and **TWO** appeared! Those weren't the snouts I'd been hoping to see. They were the bodyguards of the wicked Sewer Rat leader, Tony Sludge! Before we knew what was happening, One and Two detached the net from the ceiling. Then they grabbed us by our paws and dragged us away.

"W-where a-are we going?" I squeaked, trying not to faint.

Tony's bodyguards didn't respond. Instead they just chuckled under their whiskers.

Our journey through the sewers of **Rottington** seemed to go on forever!

We found ourselves:

1 **Bouncing** our snouts on the steps of a very steep staircase

2 **Banging** our ears on a lot of pipes

3 **Slamming** our heads against the floor of an elevator that stopped and started over and over.

Come . . .

. . . with us!

Oof!

Grunt!

Then, suddenly . . .

ONE and **TWO** stopped, and we rolled out of the net. A door closed behind our tails with a **slam**! We were alone.

"Where are we?" I whispered, running a paw over my fur to check for bumps and bruises.

"It looks like a broom closet," said *Swiftpaws*.

We were in a small, dark **room**, filled with brooms, mops, and rags.

"**CHeeSe niBLetS!**" I exclaimed, feeling a spider scurry between my paws. "It doesn't seem like this place gets cleaned very often!"

"Shhhhh! Did you hear that?" asked Swiftpaws, raising his ears.

Behind the door, I heard a **FAMILIAR** squeak.

"So, is everything ready?"

Ha, ha, ha!

I peeked through the lock in the door, and saw **Tony Sludge**, the leader of the Sewer Rats!

"Everything's ready, Boss," Slickfur told him.

Tony sneered. "Since no one will hand over control of Muskrat City, my crickets will gnaw at it until the city is reduced to a pile of dust! **Ha, ha, ha!**"

I felt my fur turn as pale as a ball of mozzarella. "We have to do something!" I whispered to Swiftpaws.

84

Swiftpaws **STARED** at the door, thinking hard.

And then . . .

"Supersuit: Super-Screwdriver Mode!"

Before I twitched a whisker, Swiftpaws had transformed into an enormouse yellow screwdriver!

"**HURRY**, Superstilton!" he instructed. "While I unscrew the door hinges, you push as hard as you can! We've got to *get out* of here—fast!"

"Rats, Swiftpaws!" I **SQUEAKED**, pushing against the door. "This door is so heavy!"

You can do it, Superstilton!

But just when I thought I couldn't possibly push anymore, the hinges

85

broke, the door **tipped** forward, and we fell flat on our snouts.

Ow!

BAM!

What superfools!

Owwwwww!

Rats!

THE DRILLING PYRAMID

When we scrambled to our paws, Swiftpaws and I found ourselves looking at an **impressive** sight. An enormouse pyramid of crickets TOWERED up to the ceiling!

Slickfur was at the top of the pyramid, and he was wearing his MASK.

Tony stood nearby, eyeing us and laughing. "Welcome, Heromice—you're just in time! HA, HA, HA!"

"Ready to help us destroy Muskrat City?" Slickfur hissed.

At that moment, a blue **ARROW** quickly whizzed past our sore snouts. By the

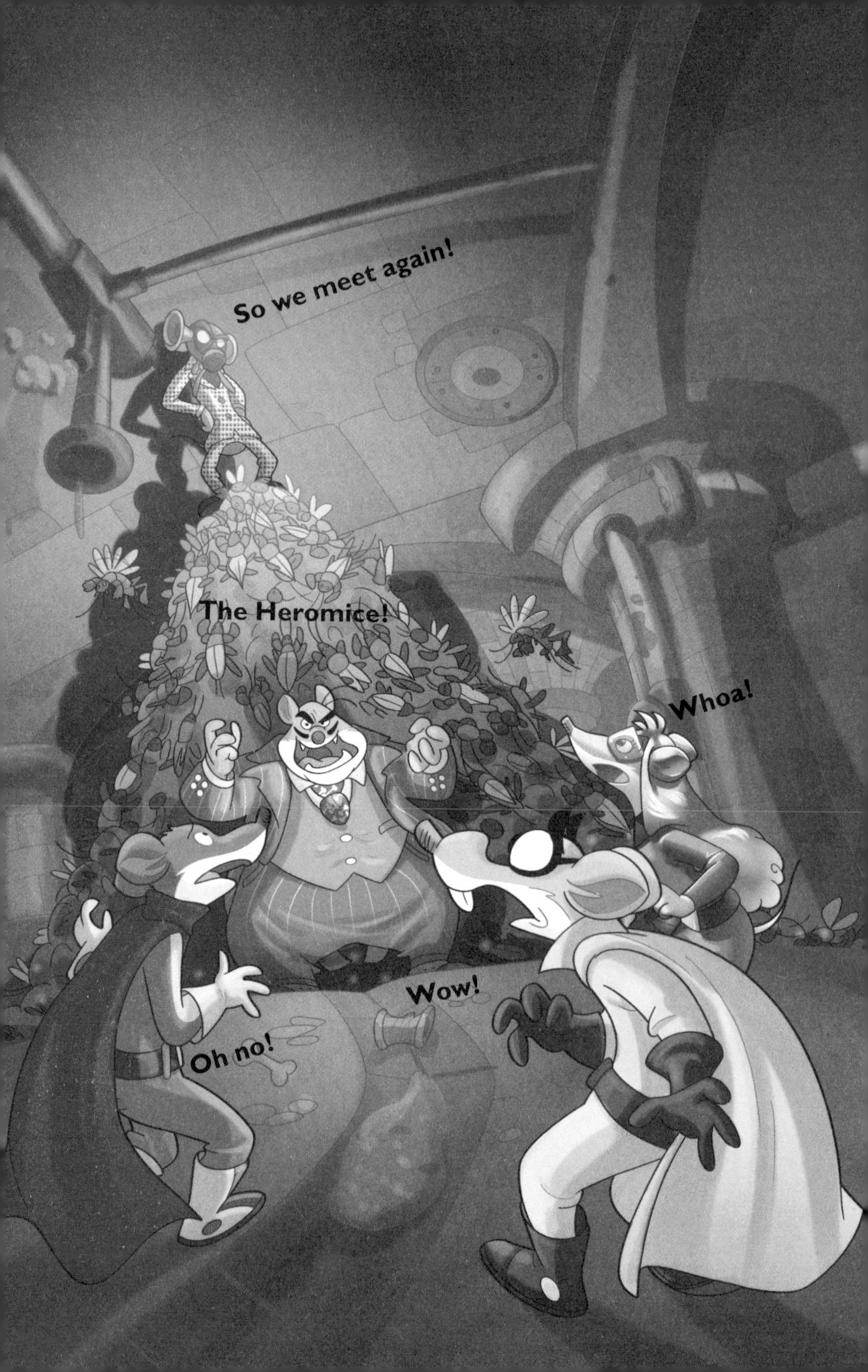
So we meet again!
The Heromice!
Whoa!
Wow!
Oh no!

power of Parmesan, it was Lady Wonderwhiskers!

Swiftpaws cheered. Then he grabbed my paw and pulled me along, leaping through the air and squeaking:

"Heromice to the rescue!"

Feeling more super than ever, we joined the fabumouse Lady Wonderwhiskers in front of the cricket pyramid. We tried to climb to the top to reach Slickfur, but the insects began to gnaw at our fur!

"**OWWWWW!**" I cried, tumbling back to the ground.

Tony stood in front of the mountain of insects, snarling at us. "There's no way out, superfools!"

Then Slickfur launched a call signal through the speakers of his mask.

"ZZZZZZZZ!"

Everything around us began to vibrate.

Swiftpaws yelled, "Super Swiss slices, the pyramid is moving!"

The swarm of insects began to **gnaw** through the sewer pipes!

We heard Tony **shout**, "Soon, this drilling pyramid will topple the bridge above Muskrat City! That is unless . . ."

"Unless what?" we cried desperately.

Tony **smiled**. "Unless you surrender and hand the city over to me."

Suddenly, a ray of light illuminated us. Holey cheese—the top of the cricket pyramid had already made a hole and broken through to the surface! The crickets were coming up right next to the support pylon of the suspension bridge!

For all the mozzarella in Muskrat City — now what?

SUPER-STOPLIGHT!

The drilling pyramid did its job, and the crickets started chomping at the cement bridge pylon. **SQUEAK!**

"They're going to make the pylon crumble!" I cried. "What can we do?"

"I have an idea!" exclaimed Lady Wonderwhiskers. "Superstilton, Swiftpaws: **FoLLoW me**!" She began to quickly climb the pyramid, using the crickets' **exoskeletons*** as footholds.

We **FOLLOWED** her, moving as fast as our paws would take us.

"Ta-da!" cheered Lady Wonderwhiskers as she reached the top of the pyramid. She

*An exoskeleton is the external supportive covering that protects the bodies of certain insects.

took a mousetastic **leap** and landed on the railing of the bridge. Swiftpaws followed her *easily*, and then it was my turn. I tried not to EMBARRASS myself, but I was a little less agile and quick than my superpartners.

Whoa!

1   First, I slipped on the EXOSKELETON of a cricket.

2   Then I lost **Ouch!** my *grip* and slammed into the railing of the bridge.

3   Finally, I was left swinging in the **air** with my paws dangling!

Eek!

Mighty mozzarella, I didn't want to land in the **river**! Luckily, Swiftpaws and Lady Wonderwhiskers GRABBED me just before I tumbled off the bridge. Superpowered Swiss, that was close!

But I didn't have long to catch my breath before . . .

CRACK!

An enormouse **crevice** opened in the middle of the road that crossed the bridge.

Lady Wonderwhiskers pointed at the approaching cars. "We have to do something *right away*, or those cars will fall in!"

"I've got it!" Swiftpaws said. "You block traffic in the other lane. Supersuit: Super- Stoplight Mode!"

He transformed into a stoplight and moved to the middle of the street, flashing a red light. The cars **stopped**, forming a long line.

While Swiftpaws stopped the cars along

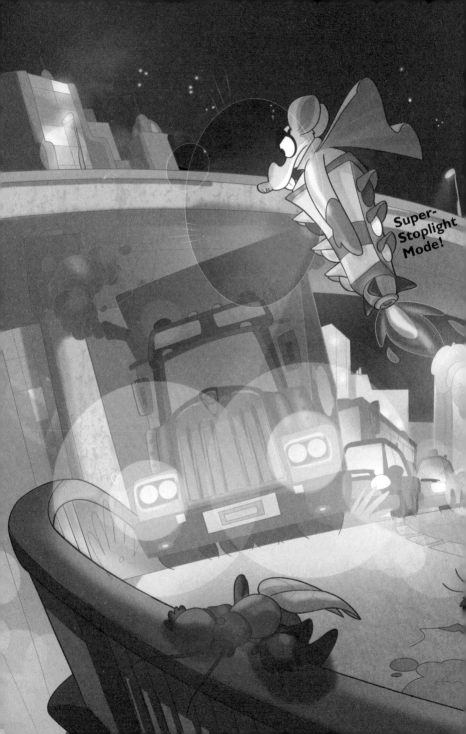

the bridge, I raised my ears, super-worried. Holey cheese — I could hear the terrible ticking of hundreds of cricket feet and thousands of cricket teeth!

We turned to find the super-insects gathered there, **buzzing** around Slickfur.

But this battle wasn't over yet!

Bogged Down in Cheese Fondue

"What do you think you're doing, **cheesebrains**?" Slickfur asked with a snarl. "This bridge is only the beginning. Soon the crickets will reduce the whole city to **crumbs**!"

The super-insects swarmed around him, waiting for more orders. *Slickfur* pointed a paw at the hills behind Muskrat City. "Destroy the aqueduct, crickets!"

"*N-n-now what?*" I whispered to the other Heromice.

Lady Wonderwhiskers looked me straight in the eye and said, "Now it's *your turn*, Superstilton."

I couldn't believe my ears! This fabumouse rodent had put all of her trust in me . . . and I didn't have a cheesecrumb of an idea of what to do!

SUPERPOWER:
RIVER OF SUPER-CREAMY CHEESE FONDUE
ACTIVATED WITH THE CRY:
"FOR ALL THE CHEESE FONDUE!"

So I yelled, "FOR ALL THE CHEESE FONDUE, it can't end like this!"

With those words, my superpowers activated! A river of **cheese fondue** flooded the bridge, flowing directly toward the swarm of crickets. The gooey cheese STUCK to the insects, holding them down. Now they couldn't fly!

Even Slickfur was trapped!

With a super-impressive leap, Lady Wonderwhiskers grabbed the mask off Slickfur's snout. "Mission accomplished, **Heromice**!"

I cheered and gave Lady Wonderwhiskers a high five, but she surprised me with a sweet **KISS** on the snout. Holey cheese! I turned as red as the sauce on my favorite triple-cheese pizza and grinned, totally **SQUEAKLESS**.

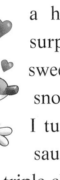

Smaaack!

Luckily, Swiftpaws joined us with a cheer. "Great job, Heromice!"

But our celebration was interrupted when . . .

Vrooooooooom!

The Sewer Rats' SLUDGEMOBILE wove through the cars on the bridge, stopping in front of us with a *screeeeeeech*. Tony Sludge climbed out.

"I don't believe it!" he bellowed. "This time you will pay, Heromice!"

CRICKET ATTACK!

Tony Sludge **STOMPED** up to Lady Wonderwhiskers, who still held Slickfur's mask in her paws.

"Leave her alone, you **rat**!" I yelled. But before I knew what was happening . . .

SPLAT!

I lost my balance and ended up falling flat on my snout in a puddle of *cheese fondue*!

When I got up, I could hardly believe my eyes. A **SWARM** of crickets had freed themselves from the fondue and started attacking Tony Sludge! He jumped back, trying to protect his **fur**. "Ow! Ow! Don't bite **me**, bite those **superfools**!"

Without commands from Slickfur and his mask, the crickets did whatever they wanted. And it just so happened that Tony Sludge's undertail turned out to be irresistible!

Shoo! Get away!

Now the only thing left to do was to bring the Sewer Rats to the police. Feeling BRAVE, I stepped up to Tony, but—

Vrooooom!

Slickfur zoomed up in the Sludgemobile and **SNAGGED** his boss right out from under my snout!

"You won't catch us, cheesebrains!" Slickfur sneered.

The motor growled and a cloud of purple smoke billowed from the exhaust pipe and darkened the air. Cheese and crackers, what a stench!

When the smoke finally cleared, the Sludgemobile was gone and the Sewer Rats had disappeared along with it.

"**Super Swiss slices!**" Slickfur exclaimed. "They slipped out of our paws again!"

Lady Wonderwhiskers **smiled**. "But the super-creamy cheese fondue plugged the ***hole*** in the bridge! And we were able to save the city from the Sewer Rats. That's the most important thing."

Swiftpaws laughed. "It's true, we **Heromice** are pretty marvemouse!"

Feeling fabumouse, I LOOKED around. Holey cheese! The crickets still buzzed here and there, but they weren't doing any more damage!

"Wait a second!" I squeaked. "What do we do with all these JUMPING insects?"

Lady Wonderwhiskers winked at me. "I wouldn't worry too much. Let's go back to Heromice Headquarters. I'll bet Tess, Electron, and Proton can help us find a solution!"

"Good idea, Lady Wonderwhiskers," Swiftpaws agreed. "LET'S GO!"

FABUMOUSE WORK, TEAM!

We went back to Heromice Headquarters and discovered that Tess had prepared a mousetastic buffet to celebrate our success.

Electron and Proton greeted us HAPPILY. "Great job, Heromice!"

"You earned a little celebration!" Tess added.

"YUM!" Swiftpaws exclaimed. "These cubes of frosted Parmesan are whisker-licking good!"

Then he tossed **four cubes** of cheese into his mouth at once.

But I couldn't get the super-insects out of my mind. "What are we going to do about

the **crickets**?" I asked, wringing my paws.

"Relax, Heromice!" Electron said. "Even as we squeak, they're peacefully flying and munching in the gardens of Muskrat City!"

GAG!

I almost choked on a **CUBE** of Parmesan.

"**WHAT?**" said Swiftpaws. "Those gardens will look like holey Swiss cheese in no time!"

"No, no, no," Proton assured him. "We made a very interesting **discovery**. The insects that you fought weren't common crickets."

"That's right!" said Electron. "They're part of a rare, specific family of Muskratian gardener crickets. They're only found near Muskrat City!"

"Muskratian gardener crickets?" I squeaked, scratching my snout.

111

File No. 893577
Muskratian Gardener Cricket

What: A rare sub-species of cricket

Where it lives: In fields and gardens near Muskrat City, where it irrigates the ground and fertilizes the soil.

What it eats: Grass, rainwater, and soil

Characteristics: Pointy feet, sharp teeth, and very sensitive antennae

"Exactly!" Electron replied. "Their eating habits are actually very **useful** for farms, terraces, and gardens. By eating weeds and **digging** tunnels, the gardener crickets create canals for **rainwater** to run through, and they help fertilize the soil!"

Swiftpaws **cheered**. "So the problem is really solved!"

I took a look at the clock on the wall. Mighty mozzarella! It was **Late**!

"I'm so sorry, but I have to go," I said, yawning.

Tess squeaked, "But you haven't eaten anything!" She started piling my paws up with food. "Take some of this home! And take three cream cheese tarts from the tray—they're still warm. Grab a spoon and a container and scoop some **fonDue** into it, too."

She bustled around, tossing some cubes of Parmesan into a paper sack and organizing everything in a wicker basket. "Here you are: *dinner* to go!"

I SMILED at her. "Thank you, Tess!"

As my supersuit *dragged* me out the window, I waved and called, "See you next time, friends!"

For a second, I thought that the flight back would be smooth. That is, until a flock of bats appeared in front of me.

Heeeeeeeeeeeeeeeelp!

Those **RUDE** bats beat their wings and tried to get at my dinner!

One of them snagged a **CUBE** of Parmesan from the basket, but I cut him off quickly.

"**ONE CUBE AND THAT'S IT!**" I squeaked.

Then I concentrated and took off at supersonic speed. For once, I landed **exactly** where I wanted to — right on my pawchair. Squeak, what a *mighty* relief!

I had missed the big game, but I could still kick up my paws and relax. I turned on the TV and flipped through the channels until I came across a documentary on insects.

After my adventure with the crickets, it was fabumousely *fascinating*!

I ate my dinner and watched the show, curious to learn more.

After revealing amazing details about every type of ant, *bee*, and **beetle**, the narrator said, "And to conclude, one last insect . . ."

A familiar image filled the screen—a Muskratian gardener **cricket**!

The narrator *explained*, "Gardener crickets are a very rare species. Those who stumble upon these little insects can consider themselves extremely lucky."

I smiled. If that was true, then I was the luckiest mouse in the world! I was awfully lucky to have fabumouse friends who were always willing to help me. With Swiftpaws, Lady Wonderwhiskers, Tess, Electron, and Proton by my side, I could overcome all my fears and act like a real hero — well, almost! After all,

NOTHING IS IMPOSSIBLE FOR THE HEROMICE!

Be sure to read all my fabumouse adventures!

#1 Lost Treasure of the Emerald Eye

#2 The Curse of the Cheese Pyramid

#3 Cat and Mouse in a Haunted House

#4 I'm Too Fond of My Fur!

#5 Four Mice Deep in the Jungle

#6 Paws Off, Cheddarface!

#7 Red Pizzas for a Blue Count

#8 Attack of the Bandit Cats

#9 A Fabumouse Vacation for Geronimo

#10 All Because of a Cup of Coffee

#11 It's Halloween, You 'Fraidy Mouse!

#12 Merry Christmas, Geronimo!

#13 The Phantom of the Subway

#14 The Temple of the Ruby of Fire

#15 The Mona Mousa Code

#16 A Cheese-Colored Camper

#17 Watch Your Whiskers, Stilton!

#18 Shipwreck on the Pirate Islands

#19 My Name Is Stilton, Geronimo Stilton

#20 Surf's Up, Geronimo!

#21 The Wild, Wild West

#22 The Secret of Cacklefur Castle

A Christmas Tale

#23 Valentine's Day Disaster

#24 Field Trip to Niagara Falls

#25 The Search for Sunken Treasure

#26 The Mummy with No Name

#27 The Christmas Toy Factory

#28 Wedding Crasher

#29 Down and Out Down Under

#30 The Mouse Island Marathon

#31 The Mysterious Cheese Thief

Christmas Catastrophe

#32 Valley of the Giant Skeletons

#33 Geronimo and the Gold Medal Mystery

#34 Geronimo Stilton, Secret Agent

#35 A Very Merry Christmas

#36 Geronimo's Valentine

#37 The Race Across America

#38 A Fabumouse School Adventure

#39 Singing Sensation

#40 The Karate Mouse

#41 Mighty Mount Kilimanjaro

#42 The Peculiar Pumpkin Thief

#43 I'm Not a Supermouse!

#44 The Giant Diamond Robbery

#45 Save the White Whale!

#46 The Haunted Castle

#47 Run for the Hills, Geronimo! **#48 The Mystery in Venice** **#49 The Way of the Samurai** **#50 This Hotel Is Haunted!** **#51 The Enormouse Pearl Heist**

#52 Mouse in Space! **#53 Rumble in the Jungle** **#54 Get into Gear, Stilton!** **#55 The Golden Statue Plot** **#56 Flight of the Red Bandit**

The Hunt for the Golden Book **#57 The Stinky Cheese Vacation** **#58 The Super Chef Contest** **#59 Welcome to Moldy Manor** **The Hunt for the Curious Cheese**

#60 The Treasure of Easter Island **#61 Mouse House Hunter** **#62 Mouse Overboard!** **The Hunt for the Secret Papyrus** **#63 The Cheese Experiment**

#64 Magical Mission **#65 Bollywood Burglary** **The Hunt for the Hundredth Key** **#66 Operation: Secret Recipe**

DON'T MISS ANY HEROMICE BOOKS!

#1 Mice to the Rescue!

#2 Robot Attack

#3 Flood Mission

#4 The Perilous Plants

#5 The Invisible Thief

#6 Dinosaur Danger

#7 Time Machine Trouble

#8 Charge of the Clones

#9 Insect Invasion